CONTENTS

❦ Lake Classic Short Stories ❧

"The universe is made of stories, not atoms."
　　　—Muriel Rukeyser

"The story's about you."
　　　—Horace

Everyone loves a good story. It is hard to think of a friendlier introduction to classic literature. For one thing, short stories are *short*—quick to get into and easy to finish. Of all the literary forms, the short story is the least intimidating and the most approachable.

Great literature is an important part of our human heritage. In the belief that this heritage belongs to everyone, *Lake Classic Short Stories* are adapted for today's readers. Lengthy sentences and paragraphs are shortened. Archaic words are replaced. Modern punctuation and spellings are used. Many of the longer stories are abridged. In all the stories, painstaking care has been taken to preserve the author's unique voice.

Lake Classic Short Stories have something for everyone. The hundreds of stories in the collection cover a broad terrain of themes, story types, and styles. Literary merit was a deciding factor in story selection. But no story was included unless it was as enjoyable as it was instructive. And special priority was given to stories that shine light on the human condition.

Each book in the *Lake Classic Short Stories* is devoted to the work of a single author. Little-known stories of merit are included with famous old favorites. Taken as a whole, the collected authors and stories make up a rich and diverse sampler of the story-teller's art.

Lake Classic Short Stories guarantee a great reading experience. Readers who look for common interests, concerns, and experiences are sure to find them. Readers who bring their own gifts of perception and appreciation to the stories will be doubly rewarded.

❧ Ring Lardner ❧
(1885–1933)

About the Author

Ring W. Lardner was born in Niles, Michigan. His mother wanted him to be a minister. His father wanted him to be an engineer. But after two years studying engineering, Lardner left college to become a newspaper reporter.

Lardner was soon working as a sports writer for the Chicago newspapers. He joined ballplayers on road trips and in their training camps. While reporting sports news for the *Chicago Tribune*, Lardner began writing the famous "You Know Me, Al" stories. These adventures of a bush league baseball pitcher became very popular when they appeared in the *Saturday Evening Post*.

Ring Lardner's stories were funny—but as he continued to write, his humor gained a sharp edge. He wrote satires that were deeply critical of 20th-century America. The first of these satires appeared in a collection called *How to Write Short Stories*, published in 1924.

Lardner's colorful characters came from many walks of American life. He wrote about baseball players, boxers, songwriters, stockbrokers, socialites, and chorus girls. He used his humor as a weapon to attack the kinds of people he considered stupid or rude or cheap.

Lardner was tall, lean, and handsome. He married Ellis Abbot in 1911 and had four sons. "He was a quiet man," wrote one friend, "who might sit in a room for three hours without saying a word."

To most of his readers, Ring Lardner was a funny man they could count on for a laugh. Only a few saw the darker side of the big fellow with the brooding eyes. They recognized that biting criticism often lurked beneath the layer of humor.

A Special Note
About the Stories

The letters in this book are a work of fiction. The letter writer—a Chicago White Sox pitcher named Jack Keefe—is a character created by the famous writer Ring Lardner. Jack Keefe and his letters home lived only in Mr. Lardner's imagination. But the baseball world they describe was once very real.

During the teen years of this century, baseball was played by many men just like Jack Keefe. Most of them were from small towns. Unlike many of today's players, almost none of them had gone to college—many hadn't even finished high school. If they hadn't made it to the major leagues, they would have been coal miners, farm laborers, or done some other backbreaking work. Getting to the major leagues was the only chance any of them had to make some "good money."

As you read through Jack Keefe's letters, you'll spot the names of several real baseball players. Some of the names you may recognize—Ty Cobb and Walter Johnson, for example. Others you may not. But, in their time, these men were also well-known in the world of major league baseball. And one of the most powerful of these was the owner of the White Sox, Charles Comiskey.

Jack Keefe may not have existed in real life. But he certainly represents a player and lifestyle that were very real in the first 30 years of this century. This player was a guy with enough talent to climb out of the "bush leagues" and make it to the majors—at least for a while.

Over the years, baseball has been played by hundreds, if not thousands, of Jack Keefes. They are as much a part of the game as all the Ty Cobbs, Babe Ruths, Mickey Mantles, and Willie Mayses have ever been.

A Busher's Letters Home

Every player in baseball's "bush leagues" dreams of moving up to the big time. The hero of this funny story is the most famous "busher" in American literature. What do you think happens when Jack Keefe finally gets a chance to show his stuff in the big leagues?

AFTER I LOBBED A FEW EASY ONES OVER, I CUT LOOSE
MY FASTBALL.

A Busher's Letters Home

September 6, 1914
Terre Haute, Indiana

Friend Al: Well, Al, old pal, I suppose you've seen the story in the paper. I've been sold to the White Sox! Believe me, Al, it came as a surprise to me. And I bet it did to all you good old pals down home. Truth is, you could have knocked me over with a feather. The old man came up to me and said, "Well, Jack, I've sold you to Chicago." Just like that.

He said, "We aren't getting what you

are worth. So you go on up to the big leagues and show those birds that there is a Central League on the map." He said, "Just go and pitch the ball. You've been pitching real good down here, and there won't be nothing to it."

So I told him that I would do the best I could. And I thanked him for the good treatment I got here in Terre Haute. They always were good to me here. Though I did more than my share, I always felt that my work here was appreciated. We are finishing the season in second place, and I've done most of it. I can't help but be proud of my first year's record in professional baseball. And you know that I'm not just boasting when I say that, Al.

Well, Al, it will seem funny to be up there in the big show. I never even visited a big city before. But I guess I've been around enough not to be scared of the high buildings, eh, Al?

This is still hard to believe. I didn't

even know that anybody was looking me over. Then one of the boys told me that Jack Doyle, the White Sox scout, was down here. Said he was looking at me when we played Grand Rapids. Anyway, Doyle must have liked my work because he wired Comiskey to buy me. Then Comiskey came back with an offer, and they accepted it. I don't know how much they got, but anyway, I am sold to the big leagues. And believe me, Al, I will make good.

Well, Al, I will be home in a few days. We will have some of the good old times then. Give my regards to all the boys. And tell them I am still their pal and not all swelled up over this big league business.

Your pal, Jack

December 14, 1914
Chicago, Illinois

Old Pal: Well, Al, there's not much to tell you. As you know, Comiskey wrote me. He said to drop in and see him. So I got to Chicago Tuesday morning. I went to his office in the afternoon. His office is out at the ball park. And, believe me, it is *some* park and *some* office!

I went in and asked for Comiskey. A young fellow said, "He's not here now, but can I do anything for you?" I told him my name and said I had an engagement to see Comiskey. He said, "The boss is out of town, hunting. Do you have to see him personally?"

I said I wanted to see about signing a contract. He told me I could sign as well with him as Comiskey. He said, "What salary did you think you ought to get?" I said, "I wouldn't think of playing ball in the big leagues for less than $3,000 a year." He laughed out loud. Then he said,

"You don't want much! You better stick around town until the boss comes back." So here I am. And it's costing me a dollar a day to stay at the hotel on Cottage Grove Avenue. That's my own money— not including my meals.

Speaking of money, I won't sign a contract unless I get the salary you and I talked of—$3,000. You know, I was only getting $150 a month in Terre Haute. And I know it's going to cost me a lot more to live here. When Comiskey comes back, I will name him $3,000 as my lowest figure. I guess he'll come through when he sees I mean business. I heard that Walsh was getting twice as much as that.

The newspaper says Comiskey will be back sometime tomorrow. You'll see, old pal. I am going to get a contract for $3,000. And if he doesn't want to give it to me—he can do the other thing. You know me, Al.

Yours truly, Jack

December 16, 1914
Chicago, Illinois

Dear Friend Al: Well, I'll be home in a couple of days now. But I wanted to write you and let you know how I came out with Comiskey. I signed my contract yesterday afternoon. He is a great old fellow, Al. No wonder everybody likes him. He said, "Doyle tells me you're pretty wild." I said, "Oh, no, I got good control." He said, "Well, do you want to sign?" I said, "Yes—if I get my figure." He asked, "What's your figure?" And I said, "$3,000 per year." He said, "Don't you want the office furniture, too? I thought you were a young ballplayer, looking for a chance. I didn't know you wanted to buy my park."

We kidded each other back and forth like that a while. Then he called the secretary and told him to make out my contract. When the secretary brought it back a few minutes later, I saw that it said $250 a month for the season.

Then Comiskey said, "You know we always have a city series here in the fall. A fellow can pick up a good bunch of money then." I hadn't thought of that, so I signed up. My yearly salary will be $1,500. What the city series brings me will be on top of that. And this is only my first year. Next year I will demand $3,000 or $4,000 for sure.

Your pal, Jack

March 2, 1915
Paso Robles, California

Old Pal Al: Well, Al, we've been in this dinky little town a couple of days now. It's bright and warm all the time here— just like June. It seems funny to me for this early in March. But I guess this California climate is all they said it was —and then some.

The hotel here is a great big place and has good eats. When the team got in at breakfast time, I headed straight for the dining room. Kid Gleason came in and sat down with me. He is kind of an assistant manager to Callahan. He said, "Hey, leave something for the rest of the boys! They'll be just as hungry as you. You shouldn't eat so much anyway. You're already overweight." I said, "You may think I'm fat. But it's all solid bone and muscle." He said, "Yes, I suppose it's all solid bone from the neck up!" I guess he thought I would get sore. But you know me, Al. I'll let them kid me now. They will take off their hats to me when they see me work.

Manager Callahan called us all to his room after breakfast. He said there would be no work for us the first day. But he wants us to take a long walk over the hills. He said we must not take the training trip as a joke.

My roommate is Allen, a left-hander

from the Coast League. He doesn't look nothing like a pitcher. But you can never tell about them darn left-handers. Well, I didn't go on the long walk because I was tired out. Walsh stayed at the hotel, too. When he saw me, he said, "Why didn't you go along with the bunch?" I told him I was too tired. He said, "Well, when Callahan comes back, you better keep out of sight. Or tell him you're sick."

When the bunch came back, Callahan never said a word to me. But Gleason came up and said, "Where were you?" I told him I was too tired to go walking. He said, "Well, maybe I should borrow a wheelbarrow some place to push you around. Do you sit down when you pitch?" I didn't get mad, Al. I let him kid me because he hasn't seen my stuff yet.

Next morning, half the bunch, mostly veterans, went to the ball park. It isn't any better than the one we got at home. Callahan asked Scott and Russell and me to warm up easy. Then they wanted us to pitch a few to the batters. It was warm and I felt pretty good, so I warmed up pretty good. I went in, and after I lobbed a few over, I cut loose my fast one. Lord was at bat. He ducked out of the way and then threw his bat to the bench. Callahan said, "What's the matter, Harry?" Lord said, "I forgot to pay up my life insurance. Hey, this is only March. I'm not ready yet for Walter Johnson's July stuff."

Well, Al, I will make them think I *am* Walter Johnson before I get through with them. But Callahan came out to me and said, "What are you trying to do—kill somebody? You'd better save your smoke because you're going to need it later on. Go easy on the boys at first, or I won't have any batters." But he was laughing when he said that, Al. I guess he was pleased to see the stuff I had.

Write soon, old pal. Tell me all the latest news from home.

Yours truly, Jack

March 7, 1915
Paso Robles, California

Friend Al: I showed them something out there today, Al. We split into two teams and had a game. One team was made up of most of the regulars. The other was made up of recruits. I pitched three innings for the recruits and shut the old birds out. I held them to one hit, and that was a ground ball that the shortstop should have gotten. I struck Collins out, and he is one of the best hitters in the bunch. I mostly used my fastball. But I showed them a few spitters, too. They missed them by a foot.

I always sit at the same table in the dining room. It's me and Gleason, Collins, Bodie, Fournier, and Allen, the young left-hander I told you about. Bodie said, "How did I look today, kid?" Gleason said, "Just like you always do in the spring. You looked like a cow." Gleason seems to have the whole bunch scared of him. They let him say anything he wants to. I let him kid me, too, but I'm not scared of him.

Collins then said to me, "You got some fastball there, boy." I said, "I was not as fast today as when I am right." He said, "Then I don't want to hit against you when you *are* right." Then Gleason said to Collins, "Cut that stuff out." Then he said to me, "Don't believe what he tells you, boy. If the pitchers in this league weren't no faster than you, I would still be playing. And I'd be the best hitter in the country."

After supper Gleason went out on the porch with me. He said, "Boy, you got a little stuff, all right. But you have a lot to learn. And you field your position like a woman. You got to hold runners on. Like when Chase was on second base today. He got such a lead on you, the catcher couldn't have shot him out at third with a rifle!" Then he quit kidding. He asked me to go to the field with him early tomorrow morning. He said he would teach me some things. I don't think he can teach me nothing, Al. But I promised I would go with him.

You should see this little blonde gal I met in the hotel. She took a shine to me at the dance the other night. But I've decided to leave the women alone. She's real society and a swell dresser, and she wants my picture. Regards to all the boys at home.

Your friend, Jack

March 9, 1915
Paso Robles, California

Dear Friend Al: You have no doubt read the good news in the papers by now. I have been picked to go to Frisco with the first team! We play practice games up there for about two weeks. The second club plays in Los Angeles. Poor Allen had to go with the second club. Callahan goes with us, and Gleason goes with the second club. Him and I have gotten to be pretty good pals. I wish he was going with us, even if he don't let me eat like I want to.

Well, Al, I will write you a long letter from Frisco.

Yours truly, Jack

March 19, 1915
Oakland, California

Dear Old Pal: They're giving me plenty of work here, all right. I've pitched four times, but haven't gone over five innings yet. I worked against Oakland two times and against Frisco two times. They only scored three runs off me. I'm not using much but my fastball. But I've got a world of speed and they can't foul me when I feel right.

Manager Callahan is a funny guy. I don't understand him sometimes. I can't figure out if he is kidding or in earnest. We rode back to Oakland on the ferry together after yesterday's game. He said, "Don't you ever throw a slow ball?" I said, "What with my spitter and my fastball, I don't need no slow ball." He said, "No, of course you don't need it. But if I was you I would get one of the boys to teach it to me. And you better watch the way the boys field their positions and hold the runners on, too."

I wondered what he was talking about. Then he said, "I noticed you taking your windup when what's his name was on second base today." I said, "Yes, I got more stuff when I wind up." He said, "Of course you have. But if you wind up like that with Cobb on base he will steal your watch and chain." I said, "Maybe Cobb can't get on base when I work against him." He said, "That's right, and maybe San Francisco Bay is made of grape juice." Then he walks away from me.

We leave here for Los Angeles in a few days. I will write you from there. This is some country, Al. I would love to play ball around here.

Your pal, Jack

March 26, 1915
Los Angeles, California

Friend Al: Only four more days of sunny California and then we start back east. On the way we got exhibition games in Yuma and El Paso and Oklahoma City. Then we stop over in St. Joe, Missouri, for three days before we go on home.

You know, Al, we open the season in Cleveland. We don't play in Chi until April 18th. I guess I'll work in that series all right against Detroit. I hope you and the boys come up and watch me as you suggested in your last letter.

Did I tell you I got a letter from the little blonde I met in Paso Robles? She went back to Detroit. But she gave me her address and telephone number. And believe me, Al, I'm going to look her up when we get there on April 29th. She is a stenographer and was out here visiting her uncle and aunt.

I will try to write you from Yuma. But we don't stay there for more than a day, and I may not have time for a long letter.

Yours truly, Jack

April 1, 1915
Yuma, Arizona

Dear Old Al: Just a line to let you know we're on our way back east. Arizona sure is sandy. They haven't got a regular ball club here, so we play a pickup team this afternoon.

This place is full of real Indians. I wish

you could see them, Al. They don't look nothing like the painted-up Indians in feather hats we saw in that wild west show last summer.

Your old pal, Jack

April 7, 1915
St. Joe, Missouri

Friend Al: It rained yesterday, so I worked today instead. St. Joe was lucky to get three hits. They couldn't have scored if we had played all week. I gave up a couple of passes, but I caught a guy flatfooted off of first base. And I came up with a couple of bunts and threw some guys out, too.

When the game was over, Callahan said, "That's the way I like to see you work. You looked better today than you looked on the whole trip." So I guess my job is cinched, Al. I would rather be in

Chi because it's near home. If they traded me to Detroit, I wouldn't care, though.

I hear from Violet right along. She says that she can't wait for me to get to Detroit. She says she is strong for the Tigers, but will pull for me when I work against them. The girl is nuts over me.

We leave here tomorrow night and arrive in Chi the next morning. That night we go to Cleveland to open up. I asked one of the reporters if he knew who was going to pitch. He said it would be Scott or Walsh, but I guess he doesn't know much about it.

Will write to you from Cleveland. You'll see in the paper if I pitch the opening game.

Your old pal, Jack

April 11, 1915
Cleveland, Ohio

Friend Al: Well, I suppose you know by this time that I did not pitch and that we got licked. Scott was in there and he didn't have nothing. It looks like Callahan means to start me in one of the games here. You know me, Al. I will give them a battle if I get a chance.

Glad to hear you boys have fixed it up to come to Chi for the Detroit series. I will ask Callahan when he is going to pitch me, and I'll let you know.

Your friend, Jack

April 15, 1915
St. Louis, Missouri

Friend Al: Well, Al, I guess I showed them. I only worked one inning. But I guess the Browns are glad I wasn't in there any longer than that. They had us beat seven to one. Then Callahan pulls Benz out and sends for me. I wasn't warmed up real good, but you know I got the nerve, Al. I ran out there like I meant business.

There was a man on second and nobody out when I came in. I didn't know who was up but I found out afterward it was Shotten. He's the center fielder. I was cold, and I walked him. Then I got warmed up good and I made Johnston look like a boob. I gave him three fastballs. He let two of them go by and missed the other one.

Then up came Williams, and I tried to make him hit a couple of bad ones. I was in the hole with two balls when I came right across the heart with my fast one. Williams hit it straight up and Lord caught it.

Then Pratt came up. He's the best hitter on their club. First, I gave him a couple of spitters. Then I came back with two fastballs, and Mister Pratt was a dead baby. I guess you noticed they didn't steal any bases, neither.

In our half of the seventh inning, Weaver and Schalk got on. I was going up there with a stick when Callahan calls me back and sends Easterly up. Then Easterly pops up. So I said to Callahan, "Now I guess you're sorry you didn't let me hit." That sent him right up in the air. He bawled me out awful. Honest, Al, I could have cracked him right in the jaw! I would have if we hadn't been standing where everybody could've seen us.

After supper I saw Callahan sitting in the lobby. I asked him, "When are you going to let me work?" He said, "I wouldn't *ever* let you work, only my pitchers are all shot to pieces." Then I told him about you boys coming up from Bedford to watch me during the Detroit series. He said, "Well, I will start you in the second game against Detroit. But I wouldn't if I had any other pitchers."

So you see, Al, I am going to pitch on the 19th. I hope you guys can be up there. You know I will be ready to show you something. I know that I can beat them Tigers. I will have to do it—even if they *are* Violet's team.

Your old pal, Jack

P.S. We play 11 games in Chi and then go to Detroit. So I will see the little girl on the 29th. Oh, you, Violet!

April 19, 1915
Chicago, Illinois

Dear Old Pal: Well, Al, it's just as well you couldn't come. By now you know they beat me. But I'm writing this so you will know the truth about the game. I don't want you to get a bum steer from what you read in the papers.

I had a sore arm when I was warming

up. Callahan should never have sent me in there. And Schalk kept signing for my fastball. I kept giving it to him because I thought he ought to know something about the batters. Weaver and Lord and all of them kept kicking them 'round the infield. And Collins and Bodie couldn't catch anything.

Callahan should never have left me in there when he saw how sore my arm was. Why, I couldn't have thrown hard enough to break a pane of glass.

They sure did run wild on the bases. Cobb stole four and Bush and Crawford and Veach about two apiece. Schalk didn't even make a peg half the time.

The score was 16-2 when Callahan finally took me out in the eighth. I don't know how many more they got. I kept telling him to take me out when I saw how bad I was. But he wouldn't do it. They started bunting in the fifth. Lord and Chase just stood there and didn't give me any help at all.

When I came in to the bench, Callahan said, "Are your friends from Bedford up here?" I was pretty sore, and I said, "Why don't you get a catcher?" He said, "We don't need a catcher when you're pitching. You can't get anything past their bats. Maybe you should leave your uniform in the dugout next inning. If you don't, Cobb will steal it off your back." I said, "Well, my arm is feeling kind of sore." He said, "Use your other one. You'll do just as good."

They batted all around in the fourth inning and scored four or five more. Crawford got the luckiest three-base hit I ever saw. He popped one up in the air and the wind blew it against the fence. You know, the wind is something fierce here, Al. But Collins should have got under it.

After Veach hit one in the eighth, Callahan called me to the bench. "You're through for the day," he said. I said, "It's about time you found out my arm was sore," I said. "I'm not worrying about your arm," he said. "I'm afraid some of our outfielders will run their legs off. And some of them poor infielders will get killed."

Well, Al, that's about all there was to it. I want you to know the truth about it. The way my arm was, I should never have gone in there.

Yours truly, Jack

April 25, 1915
Chicago, Illinois

Friend Al: Just a line to let you know I am still on earth. My arm feels pretty good again. I guess maybe I will work in Detroit. We go up there on the 29th. You can bet I will show them, Al. I will pitch the way I want to then. Them Tigers won't have such a picnic this time around, I'm telling you.

I suppose you saw what the Chicago reporters said about that game. I will have to be sure to punch a couple of their jaws when I see them.

Your pal, Jack

April 29, 1915
Chicago, Illinois

Dear Old Al: Well, Al, it's all over. The club went to Detroit last night and I didn't go along. Callahan told me to report to Comiskey this morning. I went up to the office at ten o'clock. He gave me my pay to date and then he broke the news. I am sold to Frisco.

He patted me on the back. He said, "Go out there and work hard, boy. Maybe you'll get another chance some day." I was kind of choked up so I just walked out of the office.

I ain't had a fair deal, Al. And I ain't

going to Frisco. I will quit the game first. Maybe I'll take that job Charley offered me at the pool hall. I expect to be in Bedford in a few days. I am going to lay around for a while and try to forget this rotten game.

Your old pal, Jack

P.S. I suppose you saw the story about that lucky left-hander Allen. He shut out Cleveland with two hits yesterday. The lucky stiff.

The Busher Comes Back

Jack's baseball career continues to have its ups and downs. But now a new interest has been added. In this amusing story, Jack falls in love with the girl of his dreams—and then another, and then another. How will he decide which one to marry?

"I AIN'T AFRAID TO PITCH AGAINST JOHNSON, AND I AIN'T
AFRAID TO HIT AGAINST HIM NEITHER!"

The Busher
Comes Back

May 13, 1915
San Francisco, California

Friend Al: Well, here I am in Frisco. I guess that's a surprise to you and the rest of the boys in Bedford. I remember what I told you when the White Sox sold me to San Francisco. I said that under no circumstances would I report here.

But that was before Bill Sullivan, the old White Sox catcher, gave me a little advice. He told me not to miss my chance by refusing to go where they sent me. He said, "You must remember that this was your first time up in the big show. Very few men, no matter how much stuff they got, can expect to make it first time out. All you need is experience," he said. "And pitching out in the Coast League will be just the thing for you."

So I went in and asked Comiskey to pay for my transportation. And he said, "That's right, boy. Go on out there and work hard. Maybe next year I will want you back." I told him I hoped so. But I don't hope nothing of the kind, Al. I am going to see if I can't get Detroit to buy me. I would rather live in Detroit than anywhere else. The little girl who got stuck on me this spring lives there. I guess I told you about her, Al. Her name is Violet, and she is *some* great girl.

And, of course, if I got hooked up with the Tigers, I wouldn't ever have to pitch against Cobb and Crawford again. Though I could show both of them up if I was right. They don't have much of a ball club here in Frisco, I'm afraid. Hardly any pitchers are any good, outside of me that is. But I don't care.

I will win some games if they give me any support. And I will get back to the big leagues and show them birds something. You know me, Al.

Your pal, Jack

May 20, 1915
Los Angeles, California

Al: Well, old pal, I don't suppose the home papers have much news about this league. So you may not know that I have been standing these guys on their heads. I just pitched against Oakland yesterday and shut them out with two hits. I made them look like suckers, Al.

Howard, our manager, says he is going to use me regular. He's a pretty nice fellow—not a bit sarcastic like some of them big leaguers. I am fielding my position good and watching the base runners, too. Thank goodness there aren't any Cobbs in this league. A man ain't scared of having his uniform stolen off his back.

But listen, Al, I don't want to be bought by Detroit anymore. It's all off between Violet and me. She wasn't the sort of girl I suspected. She is just like them all, Al. No heart. I wrote her a letter from Chicago telling her I was sold to San Francisco. And she wrote back a postcard saying something about not having time to waste on bushers. What do you know about that, Al? Calling *me* a busher! I will show them all. She wasn't any good, Al, and I figure I am well rid of her. Good riddance to bad rubbish, as they say.

I will let you know how I get along. And if I hear anything about being sold or drafted, you'll be the first to know.

Yours truly, Jack

July 20, 1915
San Francisco, California

Friend Al: I hope you will forgive me
for not writing to you more often. But
wait until you hear the news I got for
you. Old pal, I am engaged to be married!
Her name is Hazel Carney. She is some
looker, Al. She's a great big stropping girl
that must weigh 160 pounds. She comes
out to every game. I guess she got stuck
on me from watching me work.

Then she wrote a note to me and made
a date. I met her down on Market Street
one night. We went to a nickel show
together and had some fine time. Since
then we been together pretty much every
evening. Except when I was away on the
road, of course.

Night before last she asked me if I was
married and I told her no. She said a big
handsome man like me ought to have no
trouble finding a wife. I told her I ain't
never looked for one. And she said, "Well,

you wouldn't have to look very far." I asked her if she was married and she said no, but she wouldn't mind it. Anyway, I asked her if she wouldn't marry me and she said it was OK. I ain't a bit sorry, Al.

We are going to be married this fall. Then I will bring her home and show her to you. She wants to live in Chi or New York. But I guess she will like Bedford OK when she gets acquainted.

I have made good here all right, Al. Up to a week ago Sunday I had won 11 straight. Since then I have lost a couple. But one day I wasn't feeling good and the other day the outfielders kicked it away behind me.

I had a run-in with Howard after Portland beat me. He said, "Keep on running around with that woman and you won't ever win another game. You should go to bed at night and try to keep in shape. If you don't, I will slap a big fine on you."

So I went to bed early last night and didn't keep my date with the girl. She was pretty sore about it, but business before pleasure, Al. Don't tell the boys nothing about me being engaged. I want to surprise them.

Your pal, Jack

August 16, 1915
Sacramento, California

Friend Al: Well, I got the surprise of my life last night. Howard calls me up after I got back to my room. He told me I am going back to the White Sox. When they sold me out here, Chicago kept an option on me. Yesterday they exercised it. Howard told me I would have to report at once. So I packed up all my stuff as quick as I could.

Then I went to say good-bye to the girl. She was all broken up. She wanted to go

along with me. But I told her I didn't
have enough dough to get married. She
said she would come anyway and we
could get married in Chi. But I told her
she better wait. I promised to send for
her in October and then everything will
be OK.

I came over here to Sacramento with
the club this morning. Tonight I am
leaving for Chi. The schedule says we
play in Detroit the 5th and 6th of
September. I hope they will let me pitch
there, Al. Violet goes to all the games.
I'll make her sorry she gave me that bum
treatment. And I will make them Tigers
sorry they kidded me last spring. I ain't
afraid of Cobb or none of them now, Al.

Your pal, Jack

August 27, 1915
Chicago, Illinois

Al: Well, old pal, I guess I busted in just right. Did you notice what I did to those Athletics, the best ball club in the country? I bet Violet wishes she hadn't called me no busher.

I got here last Tuesday. I sat on the bench a couple of days. Of course, I wondered why Callahan didn't ask me to do anything. Finally I asked him why not. "I am saving you to work against a good club—the Athletics," he said. Well, the Athletics came and I guess you know by this time what I did to them. And I had to work against Bender at that. But I ain't afraid of none of them now, Al.

Baker didn't get a good hit all afternoon. And I didn't have any trouble with Collins either. I set them down with five hits, although the papers gave them seven. Those reporters don't know any more about scoring than some old woman. But I don't care nothing about reporters. I beat them Athletics and beat them good, 5-1. Gleason slapped me on the back after the game. He said, "Well, you learned something after all."

I asked Callahan if he would let me pitch up in Detroit. He said, "Sure. Do you want to get revenge on them?" I said that I did. He said, "Well, you certainly have got some coming. I never saw a man get worse treatment than those Tigers gave you last spring."

I am tickled to death at the chance of working in Detroit. Watch my smoke, Al.

Your pal, Jack

P.S. I am going over to Allen's flat to play cards a while tonight. Allen is the left-hander that was on the training trip with us. He ain't got a thing, Al. I don't see how he gets by. He is married and his wife's sister is visiting them. Allen said she wants to meet me. But it won't do her much good. I saw her out at the game today and she ain't much for looks.

September 6, 1915
Detroit, Michigan

Friend Al: I got a lot to write, but I ain't got much time. We are going over to Cleveland on the boat at 10 p.m. I made them Tigers like it, Al, just like I said I would. And what do you think, Al? Violet called me up after the game. She wanted to see me. But I will tell you about the game first.

They got one hit off me. Cobb made it a scratch single that he beat out. If he hadn't been so darn fast, I would have had a no-hit game. At that, Weaver could have thrown him out if he had started after the ball in time.

When I was warming up before the game, Callahan was standing beside me. Then Cobb came over and asked if I was going to work. Callahan told him yes. Cobb said, "How many innings?" Callahan said, "All the way." Then Cobb said, "Be a good fellow, Cal, and take him out early. I'm lame today and I can't run." I butted in and said, "Don't worry, Cobb. You won't have to run. We got a catcher who can hold them third strikes." Callahan laughed at that one. Then he said to me, "You sure did learn something out on that Coast."

Well, I walked Bush right off. And they all began to holler on the Detroit bench. "There he goes again." But then I whiffed Crawford. Cobb came prancing up like he always does. He yelled, "Give me that slow one, boy." So I said, "Coming up." But I fooled him. I handed him a spitter instead. He hit it all right, but it was a line drive that went right into Chase's hands. He said, "Pretty lucky, boy. But I will get you next time."

Cobb made their one hit in the eighth. He never would have made it if Schalk had let me throw him spitters instead of fast ones. At that, Weaver ought to have thrown him out.

When I got back to the hotel, Walsh says there have been several calls for me. I go down to the desk and they give me a certain number. I call up and a girl's voice answers the phone. I said, "Was there someone there who wanted to talk with Jack Keefe?" She said, "You bet there is. Don't you know me, Jack? This is Violet." Well, you could have knocked me down with a piece of bread. I said, "What do you want?" She said, "Why, I want to see you." I said, "Well, you *can't* see me." She said, "Why, what's the matter, Jack? What have I done to you that you should be so sore at me?" I said, "I guess you know all right. You called me a busher." She said, "Why, I didn't do nothing of the kind." I said, "You did on that postcard." She said, "I didn't write you no postcard, Jack."

We argued along like that for a while.

She swore up and down that she didn't write me no postcard or call me a busher. Well, Al, I don't know if she was telling the truth or not. But maybe she didn't write that postcard after all. She was crying over the telephone. So I said, "Well, it's too late for you and I to get together. I am engaged to be married." Then she screamed, and I hung up the receiver.

Well, Al, I must close and catch the boat. I expect a letter from Hazel in Cleveland. Maybe Violet will write to me, too. She is stuck on me all right, Al. I can see that. And I guess maybe she didn't write that postcard after all.

Yours truly, Jack

September 12, 1915
Boston, Massachusetts

Old Pal: Well, Al, I got a letter from Hazel in Cleveland. She is coming to Chi in October for the city series. She asked me to send her $100 for her fare and some clothes. I sent her $30 for the fare. I told her she could wait until she got to Chi to buy her clothes.

I also got a letter from Violet. There were blots all over it like she had been crying. She swore she did not write that postcard. She wants to know who the lucky girl is I am engaged to. I believe her, Al, when she says she did not write that postcard. But it is too late now. I will let you know the date of my wedding as soon as I find out.

Boston is some town, Al. I wish you and Bertha could come here some time.

Yours truly, Jack

September 16, 1915
New York, New York

Friend Al: I opened the series here and beat them easy. But I know you must have seen the story in the Chi papers.

Al, I told you Boston was some town. But this is the *real* one. I have never seen nothing like it. I walked down Broadway last night and I ran into a couple of ball players. They took me to what they call the Gardens. But it ain't like the gardens at home because this one is indoors. We sat down to a table and had several drinks. Pretty soon one of the boys asked me if I was broke. And I said, "No, why?" He said, "You better get some lubricating oil and loosen up." I don't know what he meant. But pretty soon the waiter brings a check and hands it to me. It was for one dollar. I said, "Oh, I ain't paying for all of them." The waiter said, "This is just for that last drink."

I excused myself because I wanted to

get some air. I gave my check for my hat to some boy. He brought my hat and I started going. Then he said, "Haven't you forgot something?" I guess he must have thought I was wearing an overcoat.

I went back to the hotel and ran into Kid Gleason. He asked me to take a walk with him, so out I go again. We went to a corner and he bought me a beer. He doesn't drink nothing but pop himself. The two drinks was only ten cents. So I said, "This is the place for me." He said, "Where have you been?" So I told him about paying one dollar for three drinks. He said, "I see that I will have to take charge of you. Don't go around with them ball players any more. When you want to go out and see the sights around town, come to me. I will steer you." So tonight he is going to steer me.

Your pal, Jack

September 22, 1915
Washington, D.C.

Dear Old Al: Well, here I am in the capital of the old United States. We got in last night and I have been walking around all morning. But I didn't tire myself out, because I am going to pitch against Johnson this afternoon.

I went to breakfast this morning with Gleason and Bodie and Weaver and Fournier. Gleason said, "I'm surprised you ain't sick in bed today." I said, "Why?" He said, "Most of our pitchers get sick when Cal tells them they are going to work against Johnson."

I said, "I feel OK. I ain't afraid to pitch against Johnson, and I ain't afraid to hit against him neither. And what is more, if you fellas get me just a couple of runs, I'll beat him."

Then Fournier said, "Oh, we will get you a couple of runs all right. That's just about as easy as catching whales with a fishing pole and an angleworm."

Well, Al, I must close. It's time to go in and get some lunch. My arm feels great. They will have to go some to beat me today, Johnson or no Johnson.

Your pal, Jack

September 22, 1915
Washington, D.C.

Friend Al: Well, I guess you know by now that they didn't get two runs for me. They got only one, but I beat him just the same—1-0. Callahan was so pleased that he gave me a ticket to the theater. I just got back from there and it is pretty late. I already wrote you one letter today. But I am going to sit up and tell you about it.

Well, first Johnson whiffs Weaver and Chase. Then he makes Lord pop out in the first inning. I walked their first guy.

But I didn't give Milan nothing to bunt
and finally he flied out. Then I whiffed
the next two. On the bench Callahan
said, "That's the way, boy. Keep that up
and we got a chance."

In the first seven innings we didn't
have a hit off of him. They had got five
or six lucky hits off of me. And I had
walked two or three. But I cut loose with
all I had when there were men on base.
So, they couldn't do nothing with me.

Then I came up in the eighth with two
out. The score was still nothing and
nothing. I had whiffed the first and
second times up. The eighth started with
Shanks muffing a fly ball off of Bodie.
He got two bases on it and went to third
while they were throwing Berger out.
Then Schalk whiffed.

Callahan said, "Go up and try to meet
one, Jack. It might as well be you as
anybody else." But your old pal didn't
whiff this time, Al. The count was two
and two. I took a healthy swing at the

next one and slapped it over first base. Bodie scored and I had them beat. And my hit was the only one we got off of him. So I guess he is a pretty good pitcher after all, Al.

We leave for home Thursday night. There ought to be two or three letters there for me from Hazel. I haven't heard from her lately. She must have lost my road address.

Your pal, Jack

P.S. I forgot to tell you what Callahan said after the game. He said I was a real pitcher now. He's going to use me in the city series. If he does, Al, we will beat them Cubs for sure.

September 27, 1915
Chicago, Illinois

Friend Al: There wasn't a letter waiting for me from Hazel. I guess she must have been sick. Or maybe she didn't think it was worthwhile writing, as long as she is coming next week.

I want to ask you to do me a favor, Al. See if you can find me a house down there. I will want to move in with Mrs. Keefe sometime in the week of October 12th. Old man Cutting's house or that yellow house across from you would be OK. I would rather have the yellow one so as to be near you. Find out how much rent they want, Al. If it is not more than 12 dollars a month, get it for me.

Your pal, Jack

October 3, 1915
Chicago, Illinois

Dear Old Al: Thanks, Al, for getting the house. The one-year lease is OK. You and Bertha and me and Hazel can have all sorts of good times together.

The series starts Tuesday, and this town is wild over it. The Cubs finished second in their league and we was fifth in ours. But that doesn't scare me none. We would have finished right on top if I had been here all season.

We will have a day to rest after tomorrow's game with the Tigers. Then we go at them Cubs.

Your pal, Jack

P.S. I have got it figured about Hazel. She must be fixing to surprise me by just dropping in. I haven't heard from her yet.

October 7, 1915
Chicago, Illinois

Friend Al: Well, Al, you know by this time that they beat me today and tied up the series. But I have still got plenty of time. I will get them before it is over. My arm wasn't feeling so good today, Al. And my fastball didn't hop like it should have, either.

But, Al, I have got bigger news than that for you. I am the happiest man in the world. I told you I had not heard from Hazel in a long time. Tonight when I got back to my room, there was a letter waiting for me from her.

You won't believe this, Al. She is married. Maybe you don't know why that makes me happy. But I will tell you. She has gotten married to Kid Levy, the middleweight. I guess my $30 is gone because in her letter she called me a cheapskate. She enclosed one one-cent stamp and two twos. She said she was paying me for the glass of beer I once bought her. I bought her more than that, Al—but I won't holler. She was no good and I was sorry the minute I agreed to marry her.

But I was going to tell you why I am happy. Or maybe you can guess. Now I can make Violet my wife. She's got Hazel beat 40 ways. She isn't nowhere as big as Hazel, but she's classier. She will make me a good wife. She's never asked me for any money.

I wrote her a letter the minute I got the good news. I told her to come on over here at once, at my expense. We will be married right after the series is over. I want you and Bertha to be sure and stand up with us. I will wire you the exact date, at my own expense.

Your pal, Jack

P.S. Hazel probably would have insisted on taking a trip to Niagara Falls or somewhere like that. But I know that Violet will be perfectly satisfied if I take her right down to Bedford. Oh, you little yellow house!

October 9, 1915
Chicago, Illinois

Friend Al: Well, Al, we have got them beat three games to one now. We will wind up the series tomorrow for sure. Callahan sent me in to save poor Allen yesterday. I stopped them dead. But I don't care now, Al. I have lost interest in the game. I have lost Violet, Al. Just when I was figuring on being the happiest man in the world!

Her answer to my letter was waiting for me at home tonight. She is engaged to be married to Joe Hill. He's the big Detroit left-hander Jennings got from Providence. Honest, Al, I don't see how he gets by. He ain't got no more curveball than a rabbit. And his fastball floats up like a big balloon.

Violet wrote that she wished me all the luck and happiness in the world. But it is too late for me to be happy, Al. I don't care what kind of luck I have now.

Al, you will have to get rid of that lease for me. Tell the old man I have changed my plans. I don't know just yet what I will do. I don't believe I will even come back to Bedford this winter. It would drive me wild to go past that little house every day. I would just think about how happy I might have been there.

Yours truly, Jack

October 12, 1915
Chicago, Illinois

Al: Your letter received. Too bad the old man won't call off the lease. I guess I will have to try and rent the house to someone else. Do you know of any couple who wants a house, Al?

They beat us bad the day before yesterday, as you probably know. And it rained yesterday and today. The paper says it will be all OK tomorrow. And Callahan tells me I am going to work.

I must close now. I made a promise to Allen, the little left-hander. Now I have to go over to his flat and play cards for a while tonight. Allen's wife's sister is visiting them again. I would give anything not to have to go over there. I am through with girls and don't want nothing to do with them.

Your pal, Jack

October 13, 1915
Chicago, Illinois

Dear Old Al: The series is all over, Al. We are the champions and I did it. I may be home the day after tomorrow. Or I may not come home for a couple of days. I want to see Comiskey before I leave and fix up my contract for next year. I won't sign for less than $5,000. If he hands me a contract for less than that I will leave the White Sox flat on their backs. I have got over $1,400 saved up now, Al. The city series money was $814.30. I don't have to worry. The reporters will have to give me a square deal this time, Al. I had everything, and the Cubs did well to score a run.

We are all invited to a show tonight. I am going with Allen and his wife and her sister Florence. She is OK, Al, and I guess she thinks the same about me. She was out to the game today and saw me hand it to them. She maybe ain't as pretty as Violet and Hazel. But as they say, beauty isn't only so deep.

Yours truly, Jack

October 14, 1915
Chicago, Illinois

Friend Al: Never mind about getting out of that lease. I want the house after all, Al. And I have got the surprise of your life for you.

When I come home to Bedford, I will bring my wife with me. Me and Florence fixed things all up after the show last night. We are going to be married tomorrow morning. I am a busy man today, Al. I have got to get the license and look around for furniture.

I am the happiest man in the world, Al. I am glad I didn't get tied up with Violet or Hazel, even if they were a little prettier than Florence.

For a girl, Florence knows a lot about baseball. She says I am the best pitcher in the league and she has seen them all. She also says I am the best-looking ball player she has ever seen. But you know how girls will kid a guy. I think you will like her OK. I fell for her the first time I saw her.

Your old pal, Jack

P.S. I signed up for next year. Comiskey slapped me on the back when I went to see him. He told me I would be a star next year if I took good care of myself. I guess I *am* a star without waiting for next year, Al. My contract calls for $2,800 a year. That's a thousand more than I was getting. And it is pretty near a cinch that I will be in on the World Series money next season.

P.S. I certainly am relieved about that lease. Everything is all OK now. Oh, you little yellow house!

Thinking About
the Stories

A Busher's Letters Home

1. Story ideas come from many sources. Do you think this story is drawn more from the author's imagination or from real-life experience? What clues in "About the Author" might support your opinion?

2. Look back at the illustration that introduces this story. What character is pictured? What is happening in the scene? Does the picture give you a clue about the time and place of the story?

3. How long ago was this story written? Think about the readers of that time. How were their lives different from the lives of today's readers? Do any of the words or expressions in this story sound old-fashioned to you?

The Busher Comes Back

1. Is there a character in this story who makes you think of yourself or someone you know? What did the character say or do to make you think that?

2. All stories fit into one or more categories. Is this story serious or funny? Would you call it an adventure, a love story, or a mystery? Is it a character study? Or is it simply a picture the author has painted of a certain time and place? Explain your thinking.

3. Is there a hero or heroine in this story? A villain? Who are they? What did these characters do or say to form your opinion?

Thinking About
the Book

1. Choose your favorite illustration in this book. Use this picture as a springboard to write a new story. Give the characters different names. Begin your story with something they are saying or thinking.

2. Compare the two stories in this book. Which was the most interesting? Why? In what ways were they alike? In what ways different?

3. Good writers usually write about what they know best. If you wrote a story, what kind of characters would you create? What would be the setting?

LAKE CLASSICS

Great American Short Stories I

Washington Irving, Nathaniel Hawthorne, Mark Twain, Bret Harte, Edgar Allan Poe, Kate Chopin, Willa Cather, Sarah Orne Jewett, Sherwood Anderson, Charles W. Chesnutt

Great American Short Stories II

Herman Melville, Stephen Crane, Ambrose Bierce, Jack London, Edith Wharton, Charlotte Perkins Gilman, Frank R. Stockton, Hamlin Garland, O. Henry, Richard Harding Davis

Great American Short Stories III

Thomas Bailey Aldrich, Irvin S. Cobb, Rebecca Harding Davis, Theodore Dreiser, Alice Dunbar-Nelson, Edna Ferber, Mary Wilkins Freeman, Henry James, Ring Lardner, Wilbur Daniel Steele

Great British and Irish Short Stories

Arthur Conan Doyle, Saki (H. H. Munro), Rudyard Kipling, Katherine Mansfield, Thomas Hardy, E. M. Forster, Robert Louis Stevenson, H. G. Wells, John Galsworthy, James Joyce

Great Short Stories from Around the World

Guy de Maupassant, Anton Chekhov, Leo Tolstoy, Selma Lagerlöf, Alphonse Daudet, Mori Ogwai, Leopoldo Alas, Rabindranath Tagore, Fyodor Dostoevsky, Honoré de Balzac

Cover and Text Designer: Diann Abbott

Copyright © 1996 by Lake Education, a division of Lake Publishing Company, 500 Harbor Blvd., Belmont, CA 94002. All rights reserved. No part of this book may be reproduced by any means, transmitted, or translated into a machine language without written permission from the publisher.

Library of Congress Catalog Number: 95-76753
ISBN 1-56103-071-6
Printed in the United States of America
1 9 8 7 6 5 4 3 2 1